Sugar Cakes Cyril

For information contact:
MONDO Publishing
980 Avenue of the Americas
New York, NY 10018
Visit our web site at http://www.mondopub.com

Printed in the United States of America
05 06 07 08 09   9 8 7 6 5

Design by Becky Terhune

Library of Congress Cataloging-in-Publication Data
Gershator, Phillis.
Sugar Cakes Cyril / by Phillis Gershator ; illustrated by Cedric Lucas.
p.   cm.
Summary: Seven-year-old Cyril, who lives in the Virgin Islands, finds his life
changed by the arrival of a baby sister.
ISBN 1-57255-224-7 (pbk.)
[1.Virgin Islands of the United States—Fiction.   2. Babies—Fiction.   3. Family
life—Fiction.]   I. Lucas, Cedric, ill.   II. Title.
PZ7.G316Su   1996
[Fic]—dc20   96-1262
CIP   AC

Sugar Cakes Cyril

by

Phillis Gershator

illustrated by

Cedric Lucas

To Maureen, for helping Cyril make friends — P. G.

To my family, friends, and to all who inspire — C. L.

Contents

....

New Baby

Cyril wasn't big, but he wasn't little, either. He was seven years old. He had just started second grade. He was glad he wasn't in kindergarten anymore. The children in kindergarten really did look little. Cyril thought they looked like babies, now that he was seven and in second grade.

It wasn't that Cyril didn't like babies. He did. Before he started second grade, his mother told him, "Cyril, we're going to have a baby soon."

"Oh, boy! When? How?" he asked.

Cyril had lots of questions. So his mother told him about chicks and kittens and puppies. "But a human baby is the best of all," she said. "You'll like having a brother or sister. The baby will be small at first, just like you were when you were born. Then, before you know it, the baby will grow up and laugh and talk, just like you do."

But the baby was taking so long to come, Cyril forgot about it.

One night, while Cyril was sleeping, Miss Elsie came over to stay with him. When Cyril woke up, there she was.

"Where's my mother?" Cyril asked Miss Elsie.

"Your mother went to the hospital. The baby decided to come when everybody was asleep. Don't worry, we'll go visit your mother right now."

At the hospital, Cyril saw his mother sitting in a big bed. He was afraid she was sick, but she smiled and said, "Come and see the baby. It's a girl. Now you have a sister."

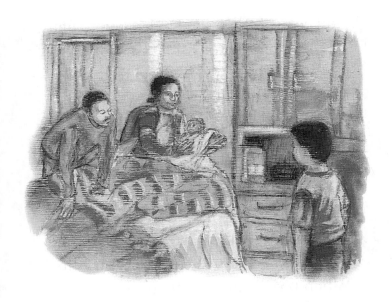

The baby was small, much smaller than he ever was, Cyril thought. She was sleeping.

"I know why she's sleeping. She kept everyone up all night," Cyril said.

His parents laughed, so Cyril did, too. But the nurse said, "Shush, you'll wake the baby."

The baby wasn't fun at all. She couldn't do anything. She just slept and cried and ate, and ate and cried and slept. Mama was always busy taking care of the baby.

"The baby eats a lot," Cyril said.

"Yes, she does," said his mother. "You did, too, when you were a baby."

"The baby sleeps a lot," Cyril said.

"Yes, she does," Mother agreed. "You did, too, when you were a baby."

"She cries a lot," Cyril said.

"Yes, she does. You did, too, when you were a baby."

Cyril made a grumpy face. "This baby can't do anything!" he shouted.

"Neither could you when you were a baby. But look at all the things you can do now. You'll see, Cyril, someday she'll laugh and talk, just like you." Mother tickled him, and Cyril couldn't help it. He giggled.

Cyril wished his parents would take the baby back to the hospital and leave her there. Some other family could have her. He had been perfectly happy without a baby in the house. Why did they need a baby around who cried a lot and couldn't do ANYTHING?

When no one was watching, Cyril went over to look at the baby in her crib.

"Stupid baby!" he said, poking her in the chest. She just gurgled and waved her arms at him.

Cyril picked up her bottle and drank all the milk, down to the last drop.

His mother came in and saw the empty bottle in his hand.

"Cyril," she said, "if you're thirsty and you want a bottle, I'll give you one, but don't drink up the baby's."

Cyril's mother filled a bottle with juice. Cyril lay down on the floor and sucked on his bottle. It took a long time to drink his juice that way, but at least it didn't spill. He couldn't lay down on the floor and drink from a cup. If he did, the juice would be all over the place.

"A bottle is very useful," he told his mother. "It doesn't spill when you drink juice lying down. I'll drink from a bottle from now on."

"Okay, why not?" she said.

So Cyril drank from a bottle, except when he was at school. The other children might not understand how useful a bottle was. They might laugh and sing, "Baby, baby, kindergarten baby! Drinking from a baby bottle. Go stick your head in gravy!"

Sugar Cakes

Since Cyril was the big brother, he was supposed to be the Big Helper. But it seemed like he was always in the way. If he poured the milk, it spilled. If he shut the door, it slammed.

And now, when he handed his mother the baby powder, he dropped it, and the top fell off. The powder spilled out onto the floor. It puffed up into the air and made them all cough.

"Go outside, Cyril," his mother snapped.

"I thought I was your Big Helper."

"I don't need a helper right now," she said, coughing. She finished diapering the baby and tried to clean up the

powder with a damp rag. "Just go outside."

Cyril sat on the porch.

"I hate that baby," he said. "I hate Mommy. I'll show them. I'll never be a helper again."

Miss Elsie passed by. She was carrying two big shopping bags.

"Good morning, Cyril," she said.

"Good morning," he answered grumpily.

Miss Elsie stopped and put the bags down. "Oh, these bags are heavy," she said.

Cyril slowly walked over to Miss Elsie and picked up a bag. The bag was heavy! He hoped he wouldn't drop it. He looked inside. Sugar. Four bags of sugar!

"I'm making sugar cakes today," Miss Elsie said. "I'm going to sell them in Market Square for the Food Fair next week. Would you like to help me make sugar cakes?"

Would he? Yes!

When they got to Miss Elsie's house, she took out two big iron pots from her cupboard and put them on the stove.

"Which kind do you like best, white sugar cakes or brown ones?" Miss Elsie asked Cyril.

"Both of them!"

"Good thing. We'll make brown ones and white ones, with coconut, of course."

Cyril helped Miss Elsie measure brown sugar and water in one pot and white sugar and water in the other pot.

Miss Elsie peeled the brown skin off the coconut meat with a sharp knife, and Cyril grated it.

They put half the grated coconut into one pot and half into the other.

"It's time to add the flavoring, ginger root and orange peel," said Miss Elsie.

"Now the sugar has to cook, cook, cook, just so—not too wet and not too

dry. You stir it up, Cyril, so it doesn't burn on the bottom."

Cyril stirred the sugar, and it didn't burn.

After the sugar cooked for a long time, Miss Elsie tested it. It was just right. She showed Cyril how to drop big spoonfuls of the boiled sugar and coconut onto a wet board.

"We have to wet the board," Miss Elsie said, "so the cakes don't stick."

The sugar cakes cooled and hardened

on the wet board while Miss Elsie and Cyril cleaned up. Then Miss Elsie gave Cyril a glass of cold hibiscus tea to drink and a sugar cake to eat.

"You're a good, good helper," Miss Elsie told Cyril. "Here's a plate of sugar cakes for you to take home."

Cyril skipped home with his plate of sugar cakes.

"You didn't want me to be your helper," he told his mother, "so I was Miss Elsie's helper. I helped her make sugar cakes for the Food Fair."

His mother broke a little piece off a sugar cake and tasted it. "Hmmm, delicious."

"I'm going to help Miss Elsie next weekend, too," Cyril added. "I'm going to sell sugar cakes at the market."

"Come," said Cyril's mother, "I'll show you how to make change. Once you know how to make change, you'll be the best helper Miss Elsie ever had."

And she showed him how to make change for a dollar when someone bought one, two, or three sugar cakes. It was easy, once he knew how.

Cyril felt so smart, he treated himself to another sugar cake.

Eclipse

"Do you think you could stay up late tonight?" Cyril's father asked him when they were eating breakfast.

"Sure, Papa," Cyril said. "I could stay up all night, if you want."

His mother laughed. "Cyril's ready to stay up all night without even knowing what you have in store for him!"

"Good thing!" Father said, "because I heard on the radio that tonight there will be a lunar eclipse. The moon will pass through Earth's shadow, starting about ten o'clock."

"That's not so late," Cyril said.

"But it takes over an hour for the moon to disappear. I only hope it's a clear night so we can see it."

Cyril kept watching the sky. "Go away, clouds!" he said. He didn't want to miss the lunar eclipse either.

That night, after dinner, Cyril helped his father wash the dishes while his mother put the baby to bed. Cyril put on his pajamas, but he didn't have to go to bed. He was no baby! He stayed up watching TV with his parents. He sat

between them on the couch, the pickle in the middle. He had almost fallen asleep sitting up when he heard his father say, "It's nine fifty-eight."

They went outside to look at the sky.

"All clear! No clouds!" Cyril exclaimed. "Wow, look at all the stars! And there's the moon." The moon was full and nearly overhead.

"One more minute now," Father said, looking at his watch.

It was ten o'clock, and the eclipse started right on schedule. Slowly the shadow covered the moon. It took about an hour until the moon was eclipsed. They could still see it, though. It looked like an orange ball.

"That's because there's still some light in the sky," Father said. "What a beautiful sight—a golden moon."

As soon as the moon was completely covered in shadow, they could hear the neighbors cheering. They cheered, too.

Firecrackers went off from a boat at sea. The sounds of shouting and clapping echoed through the hills.

Then the white light of the moon appeared again. First it was a little sliver. Then it got bigger and bigger.

It was so late, Cyril was falling off his feet.

"Time for bed," Mother said, "Now everything will happen in reverse, so you won't miss a thing."

She tucked Cyril into bed. As soon as he closed his eyes, he fell asleep. He dreamed he was on a sailing ship. There was an old iron chest on deck. When he opened the lid, the treasure inside escaped. It flew up into the sky—emeralds, rubies, diamonds, and a big coin, as round and golden as a moon shining in Earth's shadow.

Christmas Cactus

It was winter time. Winter meant the weather wasn't as hot as in the summer, but it was still hot. Winter meant it was time for the red poinsettia and white "snow-on-the-mountain" to bloom. Winter meant the trade winds blew stronger than ever. Winter meant Christmas was coming.

At school, Cyril made cards and gifts for his family. His class cut and pasted bookmarks, placemats, pencil jars, and paper plate note holders. The presents didn't cost too much money. That was lucky for Cyril because he didn't have any.

His parents said he would have

money in his pocket when he was old enough to find a job and get paid for it. But even without money, Cyril made nice presents for everybody. Now he needed a tree to put them under.

There were no pine trees on his island. Ships brought them in for Christmas from the mainland. The supermarket sold them out front, in the parking lot. Cyril loved the smell of pine trees from the north. They looked just like the trees in picture books, the way Christmas trees should. Cyril hoped his parents would buy a Christmas tree soon.

"When are you going to buy a Christmas tree?" he asked his mother.

"I don't know, Cyril," Mother said. "Those trees are too expensive. I don't think we have the money this year to buy one of those expensive trees."

"Mama! No tree?" cried Cyril. He couldn't believe it. He thought it was

probably the baby's fault, like every-
thing else that was going wrong this
year.

"Cyril, take off that grumpy face!" his
mother said. "You're good at making
things. Why don't you cut a tree out of
paper? We'll hang it up and put all the
presents underneath."

Cyril was so disappointed he ran outside. He nearly ran into Miss Elsie.

"Good morning, Cyril. I was just coming by to ask you to spray paint my Christmas tree. I'm getting a little too old to creep around among all the branches."

"Good morning, Miss Elsie. All right, I'll help you."

Even Miss Elsie has a Christmas tree, he thought. But he wondered why she wanted to spray paint it. Cyril liked his trees to look green.

Miss Elsie's tree was attached to a stand made of two pieces of wood, just like a Christmas tree, but it was not a pine tree. It was a cactus tree.

"That's your Christmas tree?" Cyril asked.

"Yes, that's what we used in the old days," Miss Elsie said. "When the century plant dies, you can cut the flower down. If you paint and decorate it, it's a Christmas tree."

"Mama says we can't have a pine tree

for Christmas," Cyril told her. "Maybe we can have a Christmas cactus instead."

"They're free for the taking," said Miss Elsie. "All you have to do is find one."

Cyril spray painted Miss Elsie's tree in the spots she couldn't reach. The tree looked shiny and new.

"Thank you, Cyril, for doing such a good job. Here's a dollar for you, and have a Merry Christmas!"

Now Cyril had money in his pocket.

He had done a job and gotten paid for it!

"Thank you, Miss Elsie. The tree does look pretty. I'm going to look for a Christmas cactus, too."

Cyril walked around looking for a century plant with a flower tree on it. He wasn't having any luck.

He told his father about Miss Elsie's cactus tree. "If we could find one, I'll buy the spray paint myself with the money I earned from a job," he said.

Father was impressed. "Well, Cyril, working for pay already? Good thing. But finding a Christmas cactus might not be easy. It takes years for century plants to make flowers, ten years at least. When they bloom, you know, they're all covered with yellow flowers. The hummingbirds and thrushes can't keep away. The birds won't point the way to a dried-up cactus flower, though. We'll have to look very hard for one."

The next day, Cyril's father borrowed a neighbor's truck. They took a ride in the country, looking hard for a Christmas cactus.

Cyril spotted one. It was sticking up at the side of the road, at least twenty feet tall. Maybe thirty feet tall!

Father chopped it down with his machete and loaded it onto the truck.

"Let's look for another one," he said, "for our neighbors. It will be just like the old days."

Cyril Sharp-Eyes spotted another, and they returned with two trees.

Cyril sprayed their tree green and gold. Then he helped his father paint the house with a fresh coat of blue paint for Christmas.

Mother made sweetbread, spice cookies, johnny cake, and holiday drinks—guavaberry wine for the grown-ups and fizzy maubi for everybody.

They decorated the tree with tinsel and glass balls. Cyril sang Christmas songs he had learned at school. Everybody had fun singing about jingle bells and snow on such a hot, sunny day.

They sang the johnny cake song, too. "Mama, bake the johnny cake. Christmas coming! Christmas coming!"

And then they sang the guavaberry song.

> Good morning, good morning,
> I wish you a Merry Christmas.
> Good morning, good morning,
> compliments to the season.
> Good morning, good morning,
> bring out the guavaberry.
> Good morning, and I wish you
> a Merry Christmas.

Father said all the singing was making him hungry for johnny cake and thirsty for guavaberry.

Mother said, "You know, Cyril made

Christmas Christmas this .year. What would we have done without our Cyril? He brought presents for everybody— the very best presents because he made them himself. And he found a tree to put them under. Hurray for Cyril!"

Cyril felt ten feet, twenty feet, thirty feet tall. As tall as a Christmas cactus.

Thar She Blows

One weekend, when Cyril and his family went to Coki Beach, his father said, "You're a big boy now, Cyril. You should learn how to swim."

Cyril looked out at the people having fun swimming in the water and snorkeling among the coral reefs.

"I'd like to swim," he said. "But I'm afraid I'll sink."

"You won't sink. Rocks sink. People float. Don't be afraid. I'm holding you. See." Cyril's father held him.

"Now stretch out," he said, "and paddle your arms like a dog." Cyril paddled his arms.

"Good for you! I'm right here," his father reminded him, "but I'm going to let you go. If I see you beginning to sink, I'll catch you."

Cyril didn't sink. He kept afloat, paddling like a dog.

"You're doing fine! You're swimming! You'll be snorkeling in no time," promised his father. "Hey, look at that crowd. What's happening?"

Cyril and his father saw people running down to the water's edge. "Let's go

see," Cyril begged, pulling on his father's hand.

What was causing the commotion? A whale out at sea!

"Thar she blows!" a man cried.

"It's a whale! It's a whale!" Everyone was jumping up and down.

From the shore, they could see the water spout shooting up from the whale's head. The spout was as tall as a tall man. They could see the whale's shadow beneath the water. The whale surfaced. It rose up and then dove back into the sea—first its head, then its huge middle, and then its tail, waving good-bye.

"It's a small whale," someone said.

It looked gigantic to Cyril.

A few minutes later it surfaced again.

By then everybody on the beach was watching the whale. A man came running out of the water. He was waving his arms over his head.

"I was right near it!" he told the whale watchers. "It was like swimming beside a huge wall. I heard the whale singing, too. It was amazing! Awesome!"

"Did you touch it?" one of his friends asked.

"I wanted to, but I was afraid of the tail. It's covered with barnacles. One swing of that tail could cut a person up or maybe even knock him out. Amazing! Awesome!"

The whale surfaced once more, farther out at sea this time. Cyril and his father watched until the whale was gone.

"Wow, that was something, wasn't it? We can't always get close to a whale," Cyril's father said, "but we can get close to a fish. We don't even have to snorkel. Come on, I'll show you. But first, we have to buy something to eat."

Father bought hot dogs at the food

stand on the beach. "Save a piece of roll," he said, "and follow me."

Cyril's father went out into the water at the rocky end of the beach with Cyril close behind. Once they were knee deep, they threw bits of hot dog roll into the water. In two seconds, Cyril and his father were surrounded by reef fish. Feeding time! The fish were almost tame. They tried to grab the pieces of roll right out of Cyril's fingers.

Cyril waved to his mother, who was watching them from under a sea grape tree. He wanted her to come and see the fish, too.

"She can't leave the baby alone, Cyril. Tell you what. We'll go and take care of the baby so your mother can go for a swim and see the fish."

"That baby isn't any fun," Cyril said. "She can't do anything."

"Well, she needs some time to grow. You don't grow up overnight, you know. Even baby chicks and kittens and pup-pies need some time to grow."

"But chicks and kittens and puppies are fun," Cyril said. "I'm glad I'm not a baby. I wouldn't have seen a whale or fed the fish or learned to swim."

"You're right. Poor baby. She didn't have any fun today, and she can't ride like this yet, either." Cyril's father picked him up and gave him a ride on his shoulders, back up the beach to the sea grape tree.

The baby was sound asleep in the shade. *Babies miss all the fun,* Cyril thought, and he kept his tired eyes wide open. He wasn't a baby, and he didn't want to miss a minute's worth of fun at Coki Beach.

Happy Face

Cyril didn't make grumpy faces as often now. Sometimes, though, he just couldn't help himself. Like when his mother and father sat on their bed with the baby and tried to make her smile and say "Mama" and "Papa."

One time Cyril told his parents, "What's the use of talking to her? It's a big waste of time. That baby can't do anything!"

Nobody listened to him. He repeated, "That baby can't do ANYTHING!" And then he shouted, "Mama! Papa!" so loudly he made the baby cry.

"If Cyril can make the baby cry," his mother said, "then maybe he can make her smile. You try it, Cyril. See if you can make her smile and say Cyril."

Cyril made a happy face for the baby. He tickled her.

She smiled!

"Look at that," Mother said. "Cyril made the baby smile."

Then the baby said, "Na, na, na, na."

"What do you know," Father said. "Cyril made the baby laugh."

"Sa, sa, sa, sa," said the baby.

"Cyril, she tried to say your name. That's the first time the baby talked!" Cyril's parents were so surprised they nearly fell off the bed.

"Before you know it," Father said, "this baby will grow up and do EVERY-THING, just like Cyril."

"Since I'm the one that made her laugh and talk, I guess I'll have to be the one to teach her some other stuff," Cyril said. "If she hurries and grows up, I'll show her how to play with toys. I'll take her to school, too, like the other big brothers do."

"Will you help teach her how to eat with a spoon and a fork and drink from a cup?"

"Sure," Cyril said. "That's easy."

And it was. When Cyril's little sister grew a little older, she copied him. She always tried to do what he did. It wasn't long before she learned to drink from a cup. Sometimes she wanted a bottle, and Cyril said, "Okay, why not? You're still a baby."

But Cyril wasn't a baby anymore. He had found a Christmas tree and seen a whale and stayed up late for the lunar eclipse. Soon he'd be starting third grade. He didn't have as much time for making grumpy faces and lying around drinking from a baby bottle now. There was too much to do. And the bigger he got, the more there was to do, like buy a sugar cake from Miss Elsie. Or better yet, make a batch himself!

Phillis Gershator is the author of many picture books, including *Rata Pata Scata Fata*, *Bread is for Eating*, and *Tukama Tootles the Flute*. She grew up in California, and has worked as a children's librarian with the Brooklyn Public Library and the St. Thomas Department of Education.

Sugar Cakes Cyril is Ms. Gershator's first chapter book. The story was inspired by real people and events on the beautiful island of St. Thomas, where she lives with her husband.

Cedric Lucas is the chairperson of a middle school art department, and his interest in art led him into illustrating children's books. Among the books he has illustrated are *Frederick Douglass: The Last Day of Slavery* and *What's in Aunt Mary's Room?* His work also appears in *America, the Beautiful*, a collection of poetry.

Mr. Lucas lives in Yonkers, New York, with his wife and two children, all of whom serve as a great inspiration for his work.